Clifford's FAIRY TAILS

SNOW WHITE AND THE SEVEN PUPPIES

CLIFFORD CREATED BY NORMAN BRIDWELL

WRITTEN BY LAUREN BISOM AND ILLUSTRATED BY RÉMY SIMARD

SCHOLASTIC INC.

Scholastic and The Norman Bridwell Trust have worked with a carefully selected author and illustrator
to ensure that this book is of the same quality as the original Clifford book series.

ISBN 978-1-338-29468-2
10 9 8 7 6 5 4 3 2 1   18 19 20 21 22
Printed in the U.S.A.   40 • First printing 2018 • Book design by Betsy Peterschmidt

Hello, I'm Emily Elizabeth, and this is Clifford, my big red dog. Every night, we cuddle up, and my dad tells us a story.

My dad loves making Clifford and me the stars of the story. Tonight we are reading *Snow White and the Seven Dwarfs*.

Once upon a time, there was a princess named Snow White. Snow White was honest, kind, and giving.

She lived in a very big castle with her very big puppy, Clifford. They had lots of adventures there.

Snow White's wicked stepmother, the queen, lived in the castle too. The queen had tricked everyone in the land into thinking she was kind and giving.

But Snow White knew the truth.

Every evening, the queen asked her magic mirror the same question:
"Magic mirror in my hand, who is most loved in the land?"
    And every evening the magic mirror gave the same response,
"You, my queen. You are the most loved person in the land."

On this night, the queen asked the mirror her usual question. However, the mirror did not reply with the usual answer.

Instead, it showed an image of Snow White and Clifford and said, "Snow White is the most loved in the land."

This made the queen very angry! "I must get rid of the perfect Snow White!" she cried.

Snow White and Clifford were playing hide-and-seek when they overheard the queen's plans. So they came up with a plan of their own. Snow White and Clifford would run away!

Snow White and Clifford escaped into the woods. The further they walked, the darker the woods became. Even with her friend by her side, Snow White was scared.

Just then, they saw a light coming from a house in the distance.

Snow White went inside the house and found . . . *a mess*! There was mud and dirt and fur everywhere. There were seven tiny unwashed bowls, seven tiny unmade beds, and seven tiny chewed-up balls.

Who lived here? She wondered.

Clifford took a sniff and let out a friendly howl. He knew who lived here!

It was seven tiny puppies!

"Hello, I'm Snow White," she said. "And this is Clifford!"

Snow White saw that each dog bowl had a name on it. She studied each pup carefully. "Why, you're Fluffy, Jumpy, and Spot," she said, pointing. "And you must be Drooly, Diggy, Fetchy, and Tiny!"

The puppies wagged their tails, happy to have made two new friends!

Snow White and Clifford needed somewhere to live, and this messy house needed some help! And so, Snow White got to work.

She ran bubble baths for Diggy, she played catch with Fetchy, and she made extra meals for Tiny.

Snow White fit right in. Clifford, on the other hand, had a little more trouble.

Snow White knew just how to help Clifford fit in!

Soon, the house was in order, and Snow White, Clifford, and the puppies became a happy family.

Every night, Snow White would tell a bedtime story to Clifford and the seven puppies. Before she knew it, they were all sound asleep.

Meanwhile, the queen was all alone at the castle. *With Snow White gone, I must be the most loved in the land,* she thought.

"Magic Mirror in my hand, who is most loved in the land?" she asked.

The mirror once again showed an image of Snow White. She was surrounded by Clifford and her new puppy friends. Snow White was even more loved than before! The queen was *not* happy.

Early the next morning, Snow White heard a knock at the door. It was an old woman selling apples as red as Clifford's fur. The old lady smiled and offered Snow White her shiniest apple.

Just as Snow White raised the apple to her lips, the dogs ran outside. They were barking and growling because they smelled trouble! But Clifford and the puppies were too late. Snow White bit into the apple, and she fell to the ground in a magical sleep.

Clifford took one sniff and knew who the old woman was. It was the wicked queen in disguise!

She pulled out her magic wand. But all Fetchy saw was . . . *a stick*! He leapt toward the queen and sunk his teeth into the wand. Lightning shot out of the wand and hit Clifford with a jolt!

Suddenly, he began to grow. . . .

AND GROW. . . .

AND GROW!

Now Clifford was bigger than ever! He let out his biggest, scariest growl. This time, the evil queen was scared! She ran away as fast as she could.

The puppies gathered around the sleeping
Snow White, and Clifford gave her a big slobbery lick.

Snow White opened her eyes. True love's kiss had broken the spell!

Snow White gave Clifford a big hug . . . or at least she tried.

And the queen? She was never heard from again.

THE END

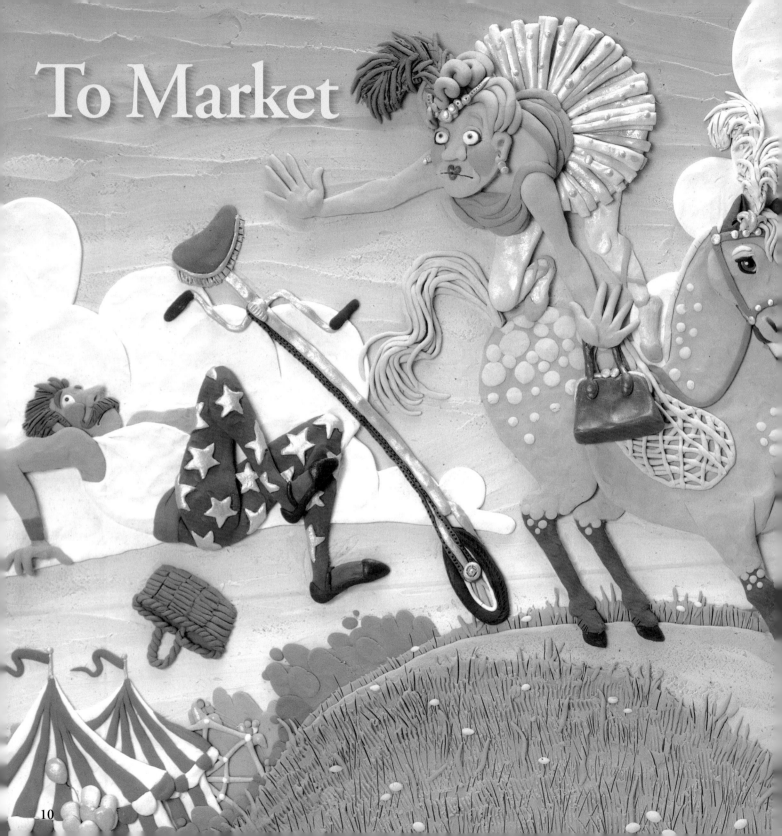

To Market

Father and Mother and Uncle John
Went to market one by one,
Father fell off, Mother fell off,
But Uncle John went on and on
and on and on . . . .

Mother Goose
Illus.: Barbara Reid

11

At the Beach

Yellow sun shines on my nose,
Golden sand burns my toes.

Silver wind combs my hair,
Orange kites dance in the air.

Bone white gulls squawk in the sky,
Saffron sea snails slither by.

Yellow starfish sleep by my feet,
Lemon ice cream tastes cold and sweet.

Blue-green sea invites me in,
Ice-blue water licks my chin.

Purple sunfish swim nearby,
Blue-grey dolphins splash the sky.

Emerald waves crash and roar,
Silver sea foam sprays the shore.

Wide blue sky hugs the sea,
Pearl-white clouds float over me.

Marie-Louise Gay

Going Up?

The high-rise I live in
Has thirty-two floors,
And eight elevators
And zillions of doors.

I live in four-eighty
And Mark in six-ten.
We visit each other
Again and again.

The superintendent,
called Adrian Box,
Lets Mark and me shovel
The snowy sidewalks.

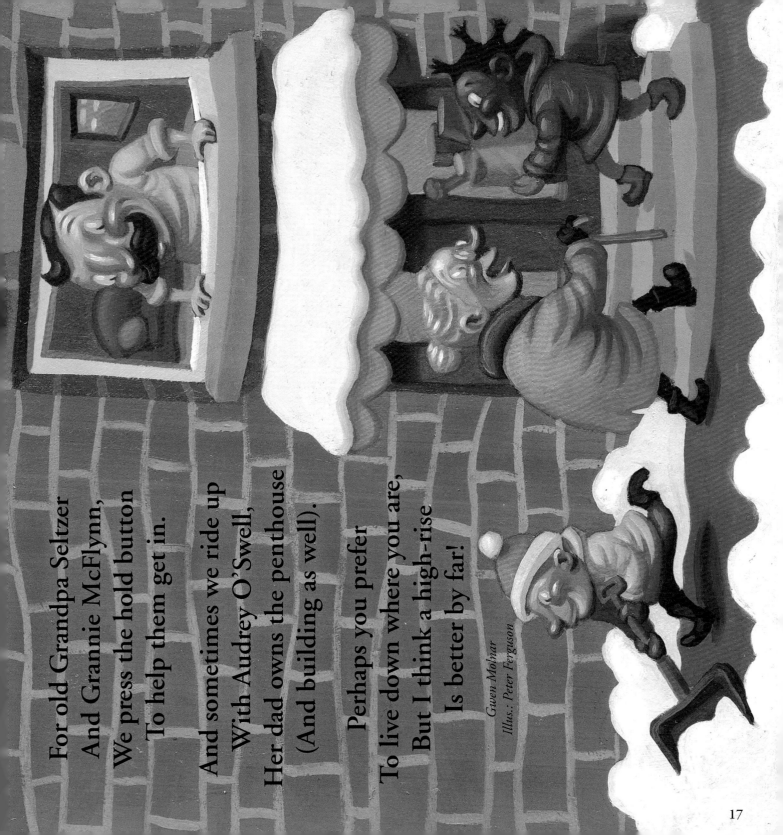

For old Grandpa Seltzer
And Grannie McFlynn,
We press the hold button
To help them get in.

And sometimes we ride up
With Audrey O'Swell,
Her dad owns the penthouse
(And building as well).

Perhaps you prefer
To live down where you are,
But I think a high-rise
Is better by far!

Gwen Molnar
Illus.: Peter Ferguson

17

Bee Dance

Bees in the ballroom, bees in the hive
Bees do the bee dance, jump and jive.
Buzz in a circle, to and fro
Promenade and do-si-do.

Swing those wings in a figure eight
Grab your partner, don't be late.
Point to the sun to find your way
Then buzz, buzz, buzz and fly away.

Helaine Becker
Illus.: Mireille Levert

Night Lights

Beneath the moon
And deep blue skies,
I count the stars
And fireflies.

One then two
Then three and four,
I hope I see
A million more.

20

They dance around
The maple tree,
And light the dark
For us to see.

I'd love to glow
And dance up high.
I wish I were
A firefly.

Sheryl Steinberg
Illus.: Stéphane Jorisch

21

Animals on Parade

This is my story,
I tell you no lies,
I saw it one day,
With my very own eyes.

A lively parade,
Marching down to the barn,
First came some sheep,
With bright balls of yarn.

Dancing and prancing,
Were three silly goats,
Wearing top hats,
And polka-dot coats.

And in their best ties,
Were two hungry horses,
Clipping and clopping,
And bringing main courses.

Blowing balloons,
Along came some ducks,
Quacking and squawking,
And pushing toy trucks.

Then looking quite pleased,
Along came the hens,
Holding up high,
Their shiny gold pens.

With chocolate cake,
Followed some mice,
Circled by birds,
All wanting a slice.

And last but not least,
Hopping down the dirt road,
Blowing his trumpet,
Followed the toad.

Where are they going,
This fun little bunch,
Do you know? Can you guess?
Do you have a hunch?

They reach the red barn,
The crowd cheers and laughs,
So happy to see,
A new baby calf.

This is my story,
I tell you no lies,
I saw it one day,
With my very own eyes.

Matthew Fernandes

Going to the Game

There's a hockey game down at the pond
and I'd LOVE to play in that.

Now… where'd my toque
and where'd my scarf
and where'd my skates get at?

Nick Thran
Illus.: Theresa Smythe

CHOOK CHOOK

Chook, chook, chook, chook, chook,
Good morning, Mrs. Hen.
How many chickens have you got?
Madam, I've got ten.
Four of them are yellow,
And four of them are brown,
And two of them are speckled red,
The nicest in the town.

Mother Goose
Illus.: Julia Breckenreid

28

29

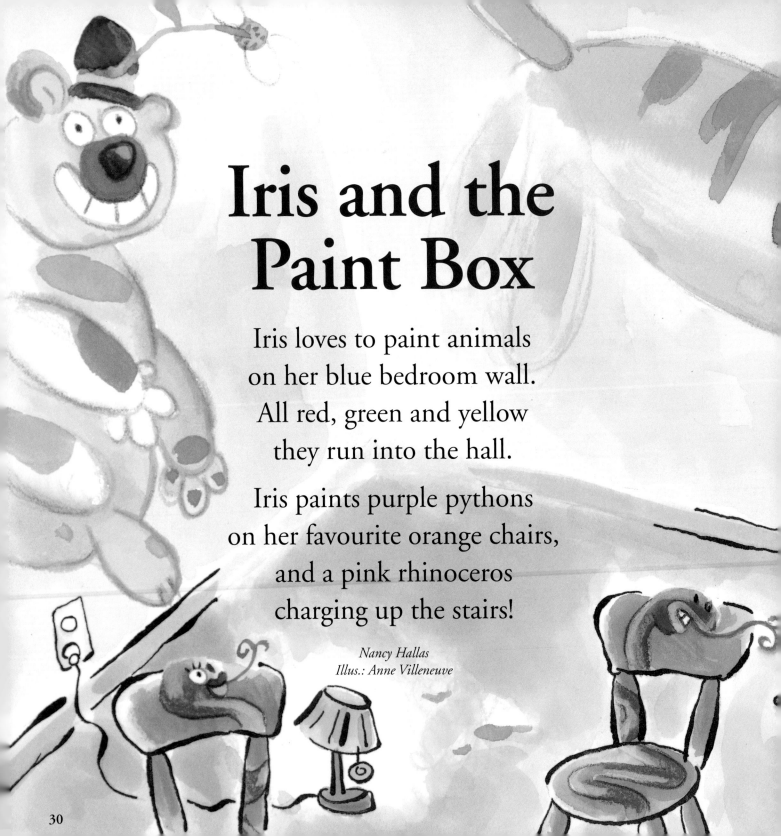

Iris and the Paint Box

Iris loves to paint animals
on her blue bedroom wall.
All red, green and yellow
they run into the hall.

Iris paints purple pythons
on her favourite orange chairs,
and a pink rhinoceros
charging up the stairs!

Nancy Hallas
Illus.: Anne Villeneuve

The Man in the Moon

The Man in the Moon
looked out of the moon,

Looked out of the moon and said,

"'Tis time for all children on the earth
to think about getting to bed!"

Mother Goose
Illus.: Dave Calver

33

Rainy Night Opera

Tinkle, tinkle, drops of rain,
Sprinkle on the windowpane.
Cymbals crashing in the sky,
Thunder sounding way up high.

Croaking, ribbit, all alone,
The bullfrog sings in baritone.
Chirping, whirring with their feet,
Crickets keep a tango beat.

Hoot, hoot, hooting from above,
The owl serenades the turtle dove.
Swooping, soaring to the tune,
They waltz beneath a smiling moon.

Toot-a-toot and rum-a-tum,
Lilies trumpet, daisies hum.
Daffodils sing high soprano,
Cabbages and corn sing alto.

Fish all dance a water dance,
Deer kick up their feet and prance.
Black crow has his head a-bobbin',
He's high stepping with the robin.

Bulrush moving in his hand,
A tabby cat conducts the band.
First soft, then loud, now sad, now sweet,
Slow it down, pick up the beat.

The willow tree forgot the words,
So hums along with the hummingbirds.
The big black bear sings out loudly,
Not very well, but he sings it proudly.

Every creature, large and small,
Every tree, whether short or tall,
Joins the patter of the rain,
To make their music once again.

Dancing fireflies, whispering breeze,
The woodlands filled with melodies.
The nighttime opera has begun,
And will go on till the rising sun.

So if some rainy night you hear,
A sound quite pleasing to the ear.
Listen close in case you should,
Hear a rainy night opera in the woods.

Debbie Ouellet
Illus.: Barbara Spurll

36

Snowflakes

Snowflakes falling one by one,
Shapes that sparkle in the sun.
Try to catch them on my tongue,
Snowflakes falling one by one.

All around us snow so white,
Makes the darkness seem so bright.
Building snowmen late at night,
And all around us snow so white.

Joanna Harvey
Illus.: Joanne Ouellet

Lick-a-licious Treat

Julie likes the red ones
but Sam chooses green.
Bree says swirly ones are yummy
and stripes are super keen.

So when the temperature is soaring,
and they just can't stand the heat,
they know it's time to chill their taste buds
with a lick-a-licious treat.

'Cause a Popsicle will cool you
on the hottest summer day.
Just be sure you eat it quickly
before it melts away!

Marilyn Helmer
Illus.: Claudia Dávila

PUSS CAME DANCING

Puss came dancing out of the barn
With a pair of bagpipes under her arm
All she could sing was, "Fiddle cum fee,
The mouse has married the bumblebee!"

Mother Goose
Illus.: San Murata

Henry Hairy

Mr. Henry Hairy had a beard so long,
His neighbour, Ms. Butter, felt something was wrong.
For how could a man whose beard dipped to his toes,
Spilled down his chest, crept over his nose,
Curled 'round his neck and covered his face,
How could he safely go out any place?
"He must be quite lonely," was Ms. Butter's hunch.
"I think I should invite this man over for lunch.
I'll feed him and clip him and then we'll have tea.
Finally, Mr. Hairy will be able to see!"

Judith Buxton
Illus.: Karen Patkau

The Spaghetti Sweater

Snick!
Snack!
Click!
Clack!

That's the sound of my Auntie Betty
Knitting me a sweater

Out of soggy, old
spaghetti.

With buttons made of **meatballs**
 And **peppers** 'round the edges,

And pockets nicely trimmed
 With **hot** salami **wedges**.

With broccoli on the shoulders
 And **mushrooms** 'round the cuffs,

And shapes made out of cheese sauce
 Or other sticky stuff.

A spaghetti sweater is kind of like
  A shirt made out of worms.

When Auntie says: "Go. Try it on…"
My body writhes and squirms.

You know
    I love spaghetti.

        I love Auntie even better.

    But I really cannot go to school
In a wet spaghetti sweater.

Every time I move
The thing will **twist** and **wriggle**,
And **silly** Sally Sutherland
Will surely point and
giggle.

HA!
HA! HA!

I could feed it to the **goldfish**,
Or the neighbour's fancy poodles,
But they'd likely turn their noses **up**
At clothing made of noodles.

That is why I'm calling you,
And the others in the bunch...

Would you like to come to my house
For a quick spaghetti lunch?

Richard Thompson
Illus.: Caroline Hamel

49

Pat-a-cake

Pat-a-cake, pat-a-cake,
baker's man,
Make me a cake as
fast as you can.
Pat it and prick it,
and mark it with a T,
And put it in the oven
for Timmy and me.

Mother Goose
Illus.: Barbara Klunder

51

Five Batty Bats

Five batty bats
Were hanging 'neath the moon.

"Quiet!" said the first.
"The witch is coming soon."

"She's green," said the second,
"With a purple pointy nose."

"Black boots," said the third,
"Cover up her ugly toes."

"Her broom," said the fourth,
"Can scratch you – that I know!"

"I'm scared," said the fifth.
"I think we'd better go."

Five batty bats
Escaped into the night.

"Dear me," said the witch.
"That's a scary sight!"

Traditional
Illus.: Howie Woo

A Sunny Land

The desert is a sunny land,
The only thing in sight is sand.
A giant sandbox, hot and dry,
It stretches out to meet the sky.

I think I'd like to go there soon,
To climb atop a lofty dune,
Or try to build a pyramid,
As high as those Egyptians did.

My camel for a trusty guide,
Upon his bumpy back I'll ride.
And in this dusty sunlit place,
I'll feel the warm wind on my face.

When I get thirsty, tired and hot,
My camel knows a shady spot.
We'll stop at an oasis green,
Where I'll refill my big canteen!

Deb Loughead
Illus.: Brooke Kerrigan

ABOUT THE COLLECTION

It was my great pleasure to select material originally published in *Chirp Magazine* for the *Animals on Parade* collection. After years of being Editor of *Chirp* and the parent of avid *Chirp* readers, I found it a daunting task. I have fond memories and strong attachments to many works that could fill countless volumes. The material selected for this collection features only a handful of the fantastic writers and illustrators who have contributed to *Chirp* over the years.

While the poems are all favourites of mine, they've been chosen to offer readers a wide variety of rhyming experiences. There are classic Mother Goose rhymes like "Puss Came Dancing" and "The Man in the Moon," and the addictive nonsense verse of Dennis Lee's "The Dinosaur Dinner." As well, the collection contains many original poems first published in *Chirp* like Matthew Fernandes's "Animals on Parade" and Sheree Fitch's "Thinking Happy Thoughts."

The selections are also intended to showcase a wide range of illustrative styles and moods. Barbara Reid's madcap Plasticine art for "To Market," and the elegant whimsy of Barbara Spurll's "Rainy Night Opera" always amuse readers. Children pore over Stéphane Jorisch's awe-inspiring sky in "Night Lights." All readers — both young and old — are enchanted by Marie-Louise Gay's watercolours for "At the Beach."

Yet, the true magic of this collection comes from the extraordinary pairing of talented authors and illustrators. Caroline Hamel's delightful illustrations perfectly capture the rollicking rhyme of Richard Thompson's "The Spaghetti Sweater." And, the energy created from the marriage of Helaine Becker's bouncy text and Mireille Levert's charming illustrations in "Bee Dance" is infectious. Our sincere thanks to all of the wonderful writers and illustrators who have shared their craft and creativity in this collection.

I hope you and your children have as much fun reading *Animals on Parade* as I've had working on it.

Mary Beth

Mary Beth Leatherdale
Editorial Director, Owlkids

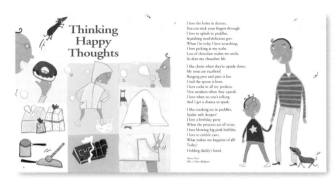

Sheree Fitch is the author of over twenty books including *Mabel Murple*, *If You Could Wear My Sneakers!*, and *There Were Monkeys in My Kitchen!* She has received the Silver Birch Award (2000), the Mr. Christie's Book Award (1993), and the Vicky Metcalf Award. "Thinking Happy Thoughts" was also published in *If I had a Million Onions*. She is a Maritimer living in the United States.

Céline Malépart received the Applied Arts Award Grand Prize (2000, 2001) and finished first in the Communication-Jeunesse Prize (2004–2005) for *Bonne nuit, Gabou!* Residing in Montreal, she has illustrated the English-language titles *Baby Ghost*, *Poof!*, *Sally Dog Little*, and *Sally Dog Little Undercover Agent*.

Dennis Lee is an award-winning poet and bestselling author of *Alligator Pie*, *Garbage Delight*, *Ice Cream Store* and *Bubblegum Delicious*. His most recent book is *So Cool*. Living in Toronto, he became an Officer of the Order of Canada in 1994.

John Berg has contributed illustrations to *The Art of Mickey Mouse* and *Garbage Pail Kids*. His work has graced many book covers, and has been featured in *OWL Magazine* and *Sports Illustrated for Kids*. He resides in Buffalo, New York.

Barbara Reid is a Toronto native who has received three Governor General's Award for Illustration nominations, winning in 1997 for *The Party*. Her unique Plasticine artwork has also won the Mr. Christie's Book Award (1991) and The UNICEF Ezra Jack Keats International Award for Children's Book Illustration (1988). This illustration originally appeared in *Mother Goose: A Canadian Sampler* as "Father and Mother and Uncle John."

Marie-Louise Gay has received eight nominations for the Governor General's Award for Illustration, winning twice for the books *Rainy Day Magic* (1987) and *Yuck, a Love Story* (2000). Based in Montreal, she writes books in both French and English. Translated into more than twelve languages, her latest works are *Caramba* and *Stella, Princess of the Sky*.

Gwen Molnar has been awarded the Canadian Authors Association Exporting Alberta Award (2000), an honourable mention from the Alberta Writers Guild R. Ross Annett Award for Children's Literature (1997), and placed first in the Canadian Authors Association Poetry Contest (1995). Living in Edmonton, she has written *I Said to Sam* and *Animal Rap and Far Out Fables*.

Peter Ferguson has illustrated *The Anybodies*, *The Nobodies*, *The Boy Who Cried Fabulous*, and the series *The Sisters Grimm*. Residing in Montreal, he has illustrated for *Business Week*, the *Los Angeles Times*, and *Marvel Comics*.

Helaine Becker won the 2006 Silver Birch Award for her book *Boredom Blasters*. She has also authored *Like a Pro*, *Secret Agent Y.O.U.*, *Pirate Power Play!*, and *Lacrosse by Knight*. Currently living in Toronto, she also wrote *Read with Chirp*, recently published by Owlkids.

Mireille Levert has won the Governor General's Award for Illustration for her books *Sleep Tight, Mrs. Ming* (1993) and *An Island in the Soup* (2001). A native of Montreal, she received a Diploma of Honour from the *Fourth Premi Internacional Catalonia d'illustración* in Spain. Her most recent English-language books are *Eddie Longpants* and *Lucy's Secret*.

ABOUT THE AUTHORS & ILLUSTRATORS

Sheryl Steinberg is a freelance writer who has been published in *Chatelaine*, *STYLE at HOME*, *Edmonton Journal*, *Rouge*, and *What's Up Kids*. Residing in Toronto, she works as a copywriter and publicist in advertising and public relations.

Stéphane Jorisch lives in Montreal and has received seven Governor General's Award for Illustration nominations, winning three times for *Jabberwocky* (2004), *Charlotte et l'île du destin* (1999) and *Le monde selon Jean de …* (1993). In 2004, he won the Mr. Christie's Book Award for the book *La boîte à bonheur*.

Matthew Fernandes received the Toronto IODE Book Award for *How Big is Big* and was nominated for the Red Cedar Book Award for *Inventions*. He has also illustrated *Farmer Bill* and *Space*. Living in Toronto, he is currently developing an animated science fiction television series.

Nick Thran has published poetry in a number of literary journals, including *Grain*, *The Fiddlehead*, *The Malahat Review*, and *Event*. Originally from Victoria, British Columbia, he currently resides in Toronto. His first collection of poetry, *Every Inadequate Name*, will be released in Fall 2006.

Theresa Smythe, with her unique cut-paper collage style, has illustrated the books *Snowbear's Christmas Countdown*, *The Runaway Valentine*, and *The Halloween Queen*. She received the Don Freeman Award from the Society of Children's Book Writers and Illustrators. She has worked on feature films and animated TV specials. A graduate of the Rhode Island School of Design, she currently lives in Los Angeles.

ABOUT THE AUTHORS & ILLUSTRATORS

Julia Breckenreid has been recognized by the Society of Illustrators of Los Angeles and American Illustration 25. Living in Toronto, she is illustrating the children's book *The Maple Syrup Taffy Tester* and is an instructor of illustration at Sheridan College. Her work has been published in *Chatelaine*, *Canadian Living*, and *Maclean's* magazines.

Nancy Hallas is the author of *The Birthday Surprise* and *Here Comes the Parade*. Her poems and stories have been published in *Cricket Magazine* and *Kidsworld Magazine*. She is currently a resident of Aurora, Ontario.

Anne Villeneuve was nominated for the Governor General's Award for Illustration in 2001 for the book *L'Écharpe Rouge,* and received the 2005 TD Canadian Children's Literature Award for the book *Le nul et la chipie*. Living in Montreal, her works have been published in *La Presse, Coup de pouce* and *L'Essentiel*. Currently, she is president of the Association of Quebec Illustrators.

Dave Calver has illustrated the *Little Genie* book series. His artwork "NYC Bling" was commissioned by the Metropolitan Transit Authority and will be featured on trains 2, 4, 5, and 6 in New York City. A graduate of the Rhode Island School of Design, he lives in Palm Springs, California.

ABOUT THE AUTHORS & ILLUSTRATORS

Debbie Ouellet has published poetry in *chickaDEE Magazine*, *Cicada Magazine*, *Asimovs*, *The Writers' Journal*, and *Tickled by Thunder*. Living in Loretto, Ontario, her next children's book, to be released in 2008, is *How Robin Saved Spring*.

Barbara Spurll has received the Mr. Christie's Book Award Silver Seal twice for the books *Emma's Cold Day* (2001) and *Emma and the Coyote* (1999). Currently living in Toronto, her latest book is *Emma at the Fair* (2005).

Joanna Harvey received the Editor's Choice Award for Outstanding Achievement in Poetry from the National Library of Poetry in 1995. A resident of Ottawa, she has previously written the *Chirp Magazine* serial "Robbie and Emily."

Joanne Ouellet received an award from the Canada Council for the Arts, and UNICEF selected one of her paintings for a greeting card. Living in Lac-Beauport, Quebec, she teaches illustration at Laval University. Her current books are *The Memory Stone*, *Solo chez Pépé Potiron*, and *Boucle d'Or et les trios ours*.

Marilyn Helmer has written over twenty different books for children. Her picture book, *Fog Cat*, won the Mr. Christie's Book Award, the Society of School Librarians International Picture Book Award, and the Toronto IODE Book Award. Born in St. John's, Newfoundland, she currently lives in Burlington, Ontario, and her latest book is *One Splendid Tree*.

Claudia Dávila has designed and illustrated numerous children's books, her most recent being *It's Your Room*, *Like A Pro*, and *Change It!* Originally born in Chile, she now lives in Toronto, and is a former Art Director of *Chirp* and *chickaDEE* magazines.

ABOUT THE AUTHORS & ILLUSTRATORS

San Murata has illustrated the books *The Boy, the Dollar and the Wonderful Hat* and *Plato and Company*. His artwork was featured in the book *1, 2, 3* published by UNICEF. He has received numerous awards from the Toronto Art Directors' Club, and his paintings have been exhibited at galleries in Toronto and Tokyo. He currently lives in Port Hope, Ontario.

Judith Buxton has received Gold and Silver awards from the Ontario Government's Information Officers Forum. Residing in Grey County, Ontario, she has written many poems for children.

Karen Patkau has illustrated eight books, three of which were selected as "Our Choice" by the Canadian Children's Book Centre. She also received the UNICEF Ezra Jack Keats Memorial Medal in 1986. Living in Toronto, her latest books are *Creatures Great and Small* and *Sir Cassie to the Rescue*.

Richard Thompson spent nine years working in early childhood education and is the author of *Draw-and-Tell*. A resident of Prince George, British Columbia, his latest series of books were written with his wife Margaret Spicer: *We'll All Go Exploring*, *We'll All Go Sailing*, and *We'll All Go Flying*.

Caroline Hamel has had her illustrations published in *The Wall Street Journal*, *National Post*, *Time Magazine*, *Reader's Digest*, *Canadian Living* and *Chicago Tribune*. Born in Quebec City and now residing in Montreal, she has illustrated the books *Autour des enfants*, *Maman s'est perdue*, and *Jano n'en fait qu'à sa tête*.

Barbara Klunder is an award-winning illustrator who has created a series of environmentally-aware T-shirts for children, and has written the book *Other Goose Rhymes*. She actively creates puppets and visuals for street theatre organizations Clay and Paper Theatre (Toronto) and Public Dreamers (Vancouver). Her posters for the Harbourfront and Vancouver children's festivals are well-known. She currently lives in Toronto and teaches at the Art Gallery of Ontario.

Howie Woo is both an illustrator and a filmmaker. Living in Coquitlam, British Columbia, he continues to illustrate for a variety of children's magazines. His illustrations can be found at www.wootoons.com.

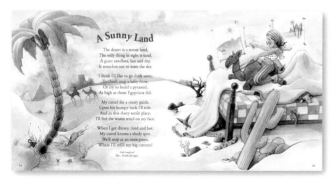

Deb Loughead has won numerous awards for her writing, and was most recently shortlisted for Storyteller Magazine's Great Canadian Story Contest 2006. She is the author of ten children's books, and coordinates the Ishar Singh Children's Poetry Contest. Based in Toronto, she is currently vice-president of the Canadian Society of Children's Authors, Illustrators and Performers.

Brooke Kerrigan has illustrated *Bullying: Deal with It!*, a Canadian Children's Book Centre Our Choice Selection (2004). She created the instruction illustrations in *Eat it Up!* for Owlkids, and her professional work has included poster and caricature commissions. Based in Toronto, Brooke is a graduate of Sheridan College.